Howard B. Wigglebottom

Learns About Sportsmanship:
Winning Isn't Everything

Howard Binkow
Susan F. Cornelison

Howard Binkow
Reverend Ana Rowe
Illustration by Susan F. Cornelison
Book design by Jane Darroch Riley

Thunderbolt Publishing
We Do Listen Foundation
www.wedolisten.com

Gratitude and appreciation are given to all those who reviewed the story prior to publication;
the book became much better by incorporating several of their suggestions:

Joanne De Graaf, and teachers, librarians, counselors, and students at:

Bossier Parish Schools, Bossier City, Louisiana
Chalker Elementary, Kennesaw, Georgia
Charleston Elementary, Charleston, Arkansas
Forest Avenue Elementary, Hudson, Massachusetts
Garden Elementary, Venice, Florida
Glen Alpine Elementary, Morganton, North Carolina
Golden West Elementary, Manteca, California
Hartsdale Avenue Public School, Mississauga, Ontario, Canada
Iveland Elementary School, St. Louis, Missouri

Kincaid Elementary, Marietta, Georgia
Lamarque Elementary School, North Port, Florida
Lee Elementary, Los Alamitos, California
Sherman Oaks Elementary, Sherman Oaks, California
Sollars Elementary School, Misawa Air Force Base, Japan
Victoria Avenue Elementary, South Gate, California
Walt Disney Magnet School, Chicago, Illinois
West Navarre Primary, Navarre, Florida

Printed in Singapore by Tien Wah Press (Pte) Limited.
First printing August 2011
ISBN 978-0-9826165-6-7
LCCN 2011934319

This book belongs to

_____

Howard B. Wigglebottom didn't like to lose.
He just HAD to be the best at everything.

At the fair, Howard won the seed-spitting contest.

He won the sledgehammer and pie-eating contests.

He won the skateboard, pogo stick, and dunk the clown contests.

As long as Howard came in first, he was happy.
But no one can come in first EVERY TIME
in EVERY THING.

Once, when Howard came in second, he threw a temper tantrum and kicked his second place trophy.

Howard even cheated friends to win.

When his soccer team made it to the
finals, he told himself that coming in
second IS NOT OK! Winning meant
everything – he was going to see to it
that his team won!

When the big day arrived …

Howard yelled at his teammates if they made mistakes.

He was a ball hog and wouldn't share.

Howard tripped a player on the other team
just as he was about to score a goal.

Then he talked back to his coach.

Time Out,
Howard!

Howard called the other team's players bad names.

He was taken out of the game.

"Howard, this is **NOT OKAY**" said the coach. "You need to learn about sportsmanship and being a team player. You are making poor choices and don't deserve to play."

Howard was the captain of the team and best player. "Coach, the team NEEDS ME to win. PLEASE put me back in," he begged. The coach shook his head no and said, "Sometimes, there are more important things than winning."

Not for Howard! "They'll lose without me and the coach will be sorry," he thought. Howard watched his teammates cheer each other on. They treated the coaches, referees, and each other with respect.

Good try!

Good job!

That's OK

Way to go
for it!

21

An upset dad was yelling at the referee. Howard watched as the man was asked to leave. "Do I look like that?" he thought to himself. In a flash, he understood how badly he had been behaving. He felt so embarrassed and ashamed.

"Please, Coach, I don't want to be like that dad," said Howard. "Please put me back in. I don't want to let the team down."

The coach nodded yes and Howard ran to join his teammates. The score was tied with one minute to go. The crowd was cheering. Howard had the ball and a chance to score the winning goal and he stopped.

Instead he passed to a teammate who took the shot and missed. Then the other team got the ball and scored the winning goal. Howard's team lost.

After the game, Howard proudly accepted his team's second place trophy. He smiled and shook hands with the captain of the winning team. "Good job." With a wink he said, "We'll get you next time."

"Howard, you can be very proud of yourself today," said his coach. "You learned about sportsmanship and were a good team player."

Howard was very happy. This second place trophy meant more to him than all his other winning trophies put together!

★ TO BE THE BEST

Howard always wanted to come in first. He used to be very upset if he lost or came in second. He felt he was better than other kids when he won a game or came in first.

Are you like Howard? Do you know anyone like him? How do you feel about losing a game to someone older than you? How about losing to someone younger than you are?

After a while, Howard learned that it is OK not to win sometimes. Winning or losing didn't make him better or less than other kids. All he needed was to do the best he could. He learned that doing his best at everything is different than being the best at everything. Can you tell the difference?

We play games and sports to have fun, to make friends, to learn new things, and to grow stronger and smarter.

It makes no difference if we win or lose as long as we have a good time and do the best we can.

★ TEAM SPORTS

Do you know what team sports means? It is when a group of kids — the players — are working together towards the same goal. That means they want the same thing, have the same target.

There are many team sports, for example: baseball, football, basketball, soccer, volleyball, rugby, polo, cricket, and lacrosse.

What is your favorite team sport? Do you watch any sports or games? Do you play any team sports or games? Can you name a few teams? Some famous teams are the Heat, the Lakers, the Yankees, the Red Sox, etc.

Before Howard learned his lesson, he was not a team player: he yelled at his teammates when they made a mistake and never shared the ball. Playing with him was not fun.

When did Howard learn his lessons? What were the lessons he learned? Howard learned his lessons when the coach sent him to the bench and he watched his friends being nice to each other and having fun. He also understood how badly he was behaving when he saw the very upset dad yelling at the refs. One of the lessons Howard learned was about being a team player.

A team player:
- is nice and respectful to his/her teammates.
- shares the ball.
- says positive things.
- forgives mistakes.
- doesn't cheat.

Do you belong to a team? Are you a team player? Playing on a team is very good for us. Do you know why? Because when we are a part of a team we learn to cooperate, to share, to solve problems, to have a positive attitude, and to work with kids that are different than we are. These are skills we will use for the rest of our lives!

★ SPORTSMANSHIP

The second lesson Howard learned was about sportsmanship. What does it mean to be a good sport? It means to:

- be fair and follow the rules of the game.
- respect all players: your teammates and the other team players, the referee, and everybody else around.
- be a good winner, be humble, and tell the losing team how well they did in the game.
- be a good loser, congratulate the winners, and tell them how well they did in the game.
- promise yourself to find out how you can do better next time.

Howard didn't want to be like that upset dad, yelling and saying bad things to the players of the other team. When Howard learned his lessons about sportsmanship he understood how to win and to lose and how to handle success and failure.

Are you a good winner? Are you a good loser? What do you do when you lose or when you win?

Remember: Sportsmanship means to be fair, have fun, have a positive attitude, and always do the best you can.

Learn more about Howard's other adventures.

BOOKS

Howard B. Wigglebottom Learns to Listen

Howard B. Wigglebottom Listens to His Heart

Howard B. Wigglebottom Learns About Bullies

Howard B. Wigglebottom Learns About Mud and Rainbows

Howard B. Wigglebottom Learns It's OK to Back Away

Howard B. Wigglebottom and the Monkey on His Back: A Tale About Telling the Truth

Howard B. Wigglebottom Learns Too Much of a Good Thing Is Bad

Howard B. Wigglebottom and the Power of Giving: A Christmas Story

Howard B. Wigglebottom Blends in Like Chameleons: A Fable About Belonging

WEBSITE

Visit www.wedolisten.com

- Enjoy free animated books, games, and songs.
- Print lessons and posters from the books.
- Email the author.